Adventures of

DANNY
AND THE
DINOSAUR

Syd Hoff

Including:

Danny and the Dinosaur

Happy Birthday, Danny and the Dinosaur!

Danny and the Dinosaur Go to Camp

Sandy Creek

Sandy Creek
387 Park Avenue South
New York, NY 10016

ISBN-13: 978-0-7607-8395-5
Manufactured in China.
Manufactured 04/2012
Lot 12 13 SCP 10 9

DANNY
AND THE
DINOSAUR

One day Danny went

to the museum.

He wanted to see what was inside.

He saw Indians.

He saw bears.

He saw Eskimos.

He saw guns.

He saw swords.

And he saw . . .

DINOSAURS!

Danny loved dinosaurs.

He wished he had one.

9

"I'm sorry they are not real,"

said Danny.

"It would be nice

to play with a dinosaur."

"And I think it would be nice

to play with you,"

said a voice.

"Can you?" said Danny.

"Yes," said the dinosaur.

"Oh, good," said Danny.

"What can we do?"

"I can take you for a ride,"

said the dinosaur.

He put his head down

so Danny could

get on him.

13

"Let's go!" said Danny.

14

A policeman stared at them.

He had never seen a dinosaur stop

for a red light.

The dinosaur was so tall Danny had
to hold up the ropes for him.

"Look out!" said Danny.

17

"Bow wow!" said a dog.

"He thinks you are a car," said Danny.

"Go away, dog. We are not a car."

18

"I can make a noise like a car,"

said the dinosaur.

"Honk! Honk! Honk!"

"What big rocks,"

said the dinosaur.

"They are not rocks," said Danny.

"They are buildings."

"I love to climb,"

said the dinosaur.

"Down, boy!" said Danny.

21

The dinosaur had to be very careful
not to knock over houses or stores
with his long tail.

Some people were
waiting for a bus.
They rode on the
dinosaur's tail instead.

23

"All who want
to cross the street
may walk on my back,"
said the dinosaur.

"It's very nice of you to help me
with my bundles," said a lady.

Danny and the dinosaur went

all over town and had lots of fun.

"It's good to take

an hour or two off

after a hundred million years,"

said the dinosaur.

26

They even looked at

the ball game.

"Hit the ball,"

said Danny.

"Hit a home run,"

said the dinosaur.

27

"I wish we had a boat,"

said Danny.

"Who needs a boat?

I can swim,"

said the dinosaur.

"Toot, toot!"

went the boats.

"Toot, toot!" went Danny

and the dinosaur.

29

"Oh, what lovely green grass!"

said the dinosaur.

"I haven't eaten any of that

for a very long time."

"Wait," said Danny.

"See what it says."

30

They both had ice cream instead.

"Let's go to the zoo

and see the animals," said Danny.

32

Everybody came running

to see the dinosaur.

Nobody stayed to see

the lions.

Nobody stayed to see

the elephants.

35

Nobody stayed to see

the monkeys.

36

And nobody stayed to see
the seals,

giraffes or hippos,

either.

"Please go away

so the animals

will get looked at,"

said the zoo man.

"Let's find my friends,"

said Danny.

"Very well,"

said the dinosaur.

39

"There they are," said Danny.

"Why, it's Danny
riding on a dinosaur,"
said a child.

"Maybe he'll give us a ride."

"May we have a ride?"

asked the children.

"I'd be delighted,"

said the dinosaur.

"Hold on tight," said Danny.

41

Around and around

the block ran the dinosaur,

faster and faster and faster.

"This is better than

a merry-go-round,"

the children said.

The dinosaur was
out of breath.
"Teach him tricks,"
said the children.

44

Danny taught the dinosaur

how to shake hands.

"Can you roll over on your back?"

asked the children.

"That's easy,"

said the dinosaur.

"He's smart," said Danny,

patting the dinosaur.

46

"Let's play hide and seek,"

said the children.

"How do you play it?"

said the dinosaur.

"We hide and you try

to find us," said Danny.

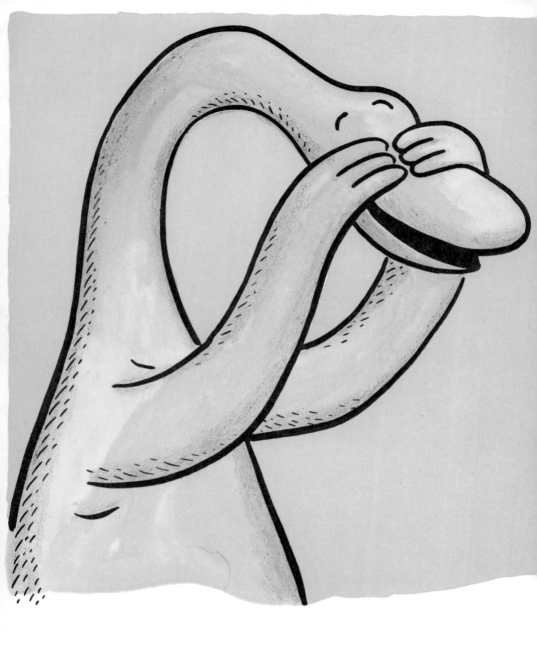

The dinosaur covered

his eyes.

All the children ran

to hide.

The dinosaur

looked and looked

but he couldn't find the children.

"I give up," he said.

50

Now it was the dinosaur's turn

to hide.

The children covered their eyes.

The dinosaur hid

behind a house.

The children found him.

52

He hid behind a sign.

The children

found him.

He hid behind a big gas tank.

The children found him.

They found him again

and again and again.

"I guess there's no place

for me to hide,"

said the dinosaur.

"Let's make believe

we can't find him," Danny said.

"Where can he be?

Where, oh, where is that dinosaur?

Where did he go?

We give up," said the children.

"Here I am," said the dinosaur.

"The dinosaur wins,"

said the children.

"We couldn't find him.

He fooled us."

"Hurrah for the dinosaur!"

the children cried.

"Hurray! Hurray!"

It got late and

the other children left.

Danny and the dinosaur

were alone.

"Well, goodbye, Danny,"

said the dinosaur.

"Can't you come

and stay with me?"

said Danny.

"We could have fun."

"No," said the dinosaur.

"I've had a good time—

the best I've had

in a hundred million years.

But now I must get back

to the museum.

They need me there."

"Oh," said Danny.

"Well, goodbye."

61

Danny watched

until the long tail

was out of sight.

Then he went home alone.

"Oh, well," thought Danny,

"we don't have room

for a pet that size, anyway.

But we did have

a wonderful day."

Happy Birthday, DANNY and the DINOSAUR!

For Bonnie

Danny was in a hurry.

He had to see his friend

the dinosaur.

"I'm six years old today,"

said Danny.

"Will you come

to my birthday party?"

"I would be delighted,"

said the dinosaur.

Danny rode the dinosaur

out of the museum.

On the way

they picked up Danny's friends.

"Today I'm a hundred million years

and one day old," said the dinosaur.

"Then it can be your party too!"

said Danny.

The children helped Danny's father

hang up balloons.

"See, I can help too,"

said the dinosaur.

Danny's mother gave out party hats.

"How do I look?"

asked the dinosaur.

79

"We would like to sing a song,"
said a girl and a boy.

They sang,

and everybody clapped their hands.

81

"I can sing too," said the dinosaur.

He sang,

and everybody covered their ears.

"Let's play pin the tail

on the donkey," said Danny.

The dinosaur pinned the tail

on himself!

The children sat down to rest.

"Please don't put your feet

on the furniture," said Danny.

The dinosaur put his feet

out the window.

Danny's mother and father

gave each child

a dish of ice cream.

They had to give the dinosaur

more!

"Here comes the birthday cake!"

said the children.

They counted the candles.

"One, two, three, four, five, six."

The dinosaur started to eat

the cake.

"Wait!" said Danny.

"First we have to make a wish!"

"I wish we can all be together again
next year," said Danny.

"I wish the same thing,"
said the dinosaur.

They blew out the candles.

"Happy birthday to you!"

everybody sang.

95

"This is the best birthday party
I have ever had," said Danny.

"Me too," said the dinosaur.

DANNY and the DINOSAUR Go to Camp

For Sally

Danny went to camp

for the summer.

He took along his friend

the dinosaur.

101

"Camp is fun.

You will enjoy it," said Danny.

"Thanks. I needed a vacation,"

said the dinosaur.

"Welcome," said the camp owner.

"You're the first dinosaur

we ever had here."

103

Lana the leader said,

"Let's start with a race.

On your mark, get set, go!"

The dinosaur took a step.

"You win!" shouted Danny.

The children played football.

The dinosaur ran with the ball,

and nobody could stop him.

"Touchdown!" shouted Danny.

Lana took everybody to the lake.

"Here is where we row our boats,"

she said.

The children rowed little boats.

Danny rowed the dinosaur.

It was time for lunch.

"Please pass the ketchup,"

said Danny.

"Of course, just as soon as

I finish this bottle,"

said the dinosaur.

After lunch

everybody wrote letters home.

"Please send me my own ketchup,"

Danny wrote.

"Send me a pizza,"

wrote the dinosaur.

113

"Now let's go on a hike,"

said Lana,

114

and everybody followed her.

Then Danny got tired

and climbed on the dinosaur.

"Wait for us!

We're tired too!"

shouted the children.

"Hold tight," said the dinosaur.

The dinosaur even carried Lana!

It got dark.

Everybody sat around the campfire.

Lana gave out toasted marshmallows.

"Here, have all you want,"

she said.

"Thanks, but I don't have room

for more," said Danny.

"I have room,"

said the dinosaur.

It was time for bed.

"I can't wait to get

under the covers,"

said Danny.

"Me too," said the dinosaur.

But the dinosaur's bunk

was too small for him.

126

He took a pillow

and went outside.

"Wake me up for breakfast,"

said the dinosaur,

and he fell asleep on the ground.

"Good night," Danny said.

128